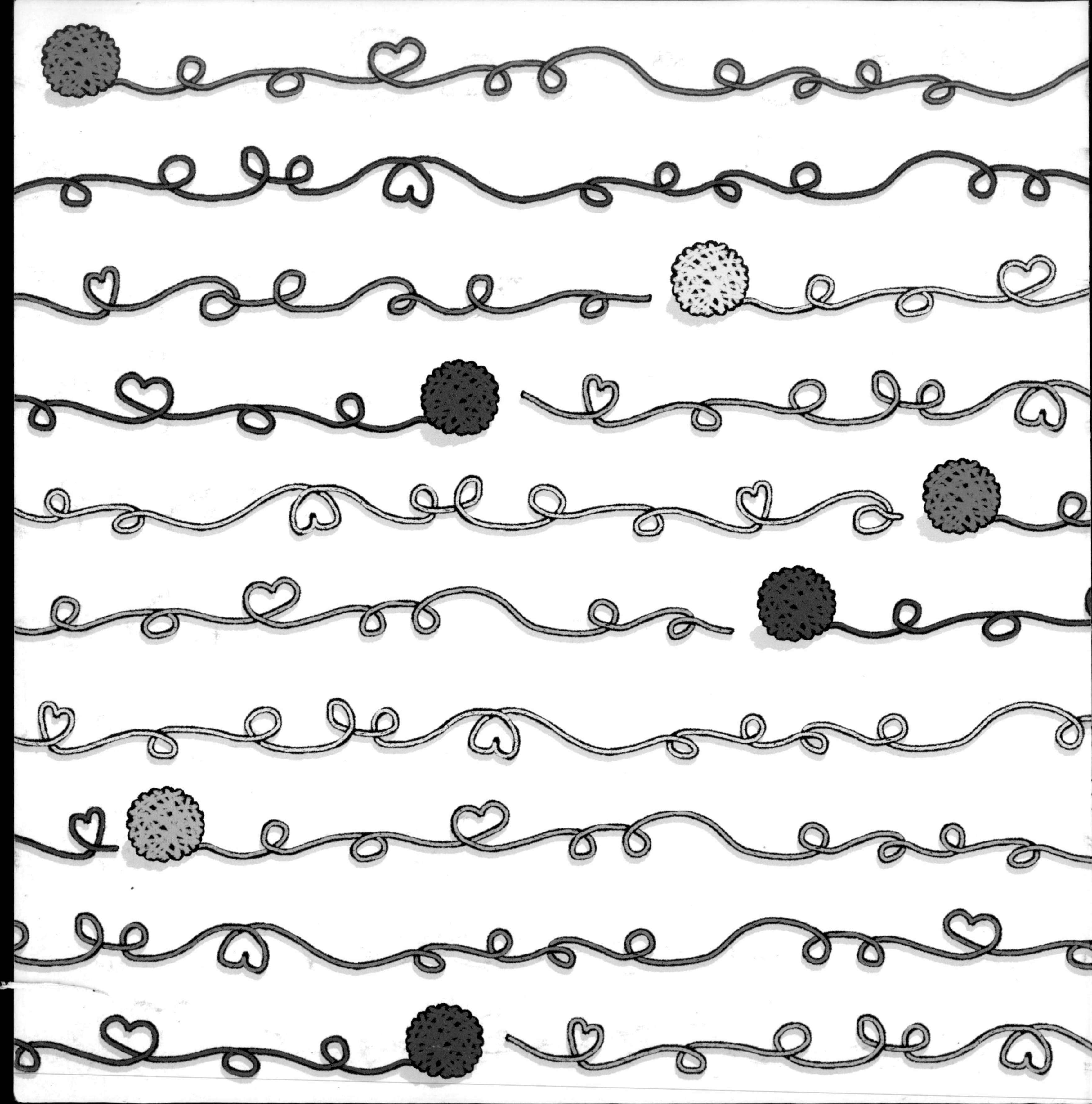

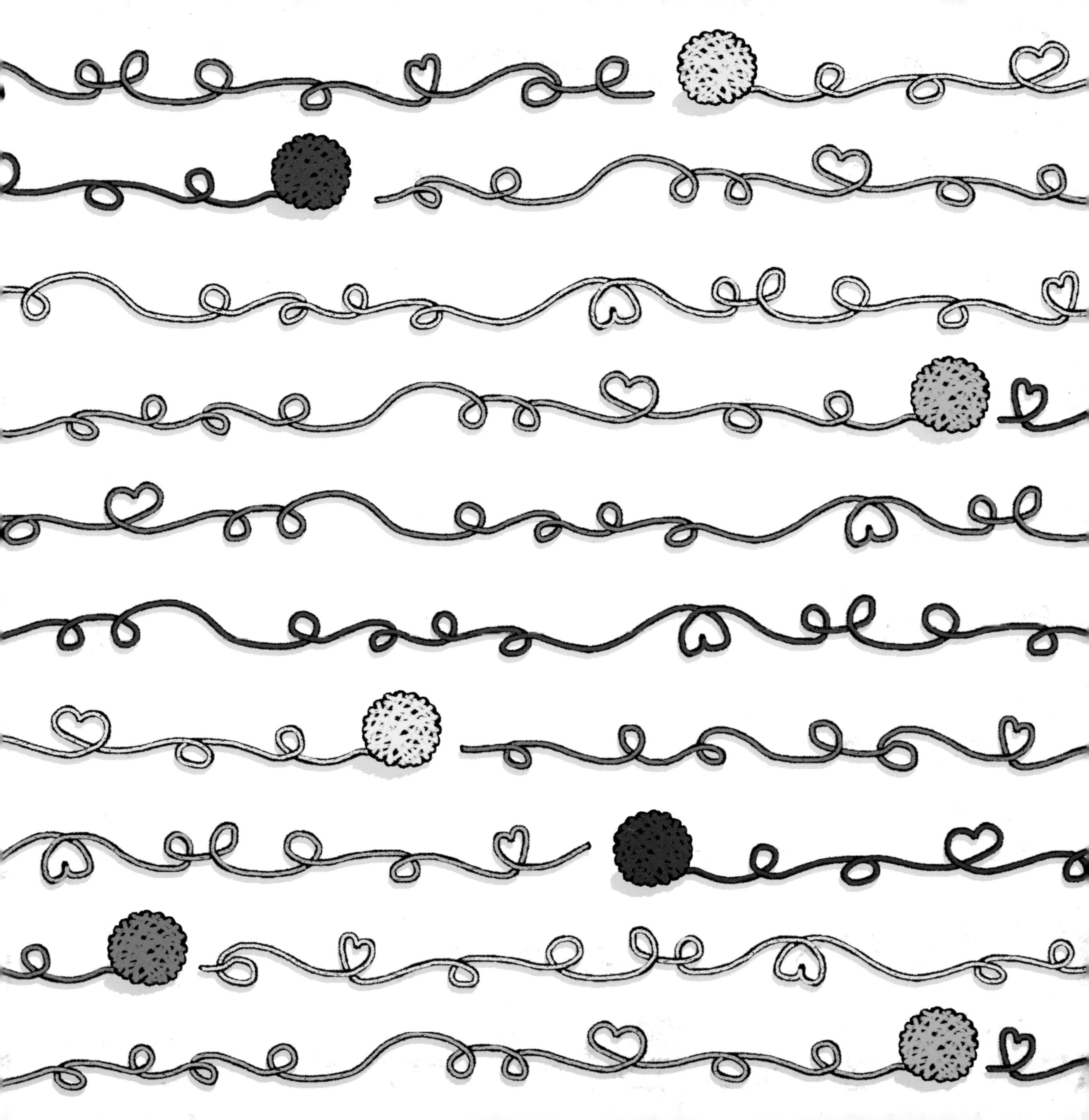

For Umma, whose love knows no bounds

Bloomsbury Publishing, London, New Delhi, New York and Sydney

First published in the United States of America in 2013 by
Walker Books for Young Readers, an imprint of Bloomsbury Publishing Plc,
1385 Broadway, New York, New York 10018

This edition first published in Great Britain in 2013 by Bloomsbury Publishing Plc,
50 Bedford Square, London, WC1B 3DP

A CIP catalogue record for this book is available from the British Library

ISBN 978 1 4088 5120 3 (PB)
ISBN 978 1 4088 5119 7 (eBook)

Printed in China by C&C Offset Printing Co Ltd, Shenzhen, Guangdong

1 3 5 7 9 10 8 6 4 2

www.bloomsbury.com

Penguin in Love

Salina Yoon

BLOOMSBURY
LONDON NEW DELHI NEW YORK SYDNEY

One day, Penguin was looking for love.

What's this?

Instead, he found . . .

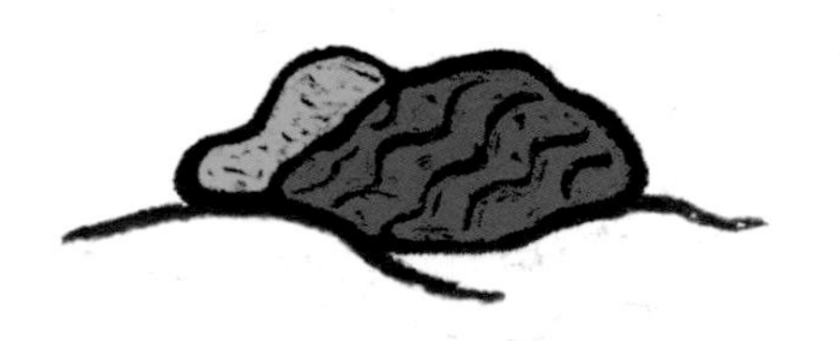

. . . a mitten.

It was a mystery.

Penguin asked Grandpa if it was his.

'No, Penguin. I like to wear hats.'

Penguin searched for its owner.

Emily was missing a bead, but not a mitten.

Isabelle was missing a slipper, but not a mitten.

Oliver was missing the sun, but not a mitten.

Penguin wondered who had knitted such a fine mitten.

Meanwhile, Penguin's friend
Bootsy was busy knitting cozies.

Knitting warmed her lonely heart.

Penguin was busy knitting, too.

Just then, a couple of puffins from out of town flew down.

'H-h-hello. A-a-are you knitting a bill cozy?' asked the shivering puffin.

'I d-d-dropped mine passing through.'

The puffin beamed with delight when Penguin gave it to him.

'Thank you!' said the grateful lovebirds.

The puffins hatched a secret plan to help the penguin find his own perfect match.

'What a perfect pair,' thought Penguin.

'This bill cozy will make a nice hat,' he said to the seal pup. 'Wait here, and I'll knit you a scarf!'

On the other side of the ice, a cold visitor asked Bootsy for a favour.

'Could you knit me a sweater?' asked the whale. This was a BIG job, but Bootsy wanted to try.

When Bootsy reached for her basket, all her wool was missing.

Penguin noticed his knitting box was empty, too.

The penguins went on a search.

'Have you seen my wool?' asked Bootsy.
'No,' said Penguin. 'I'm missing mine, too!'

Penguin and Bootsy set off to unravel the mystery together.

As they looked, they knitted for warmth.

They knitted for fun.

They knitted for comfort.

And this made Penguin and Bootsy very happy, until . . .

. . . a blizzard came and
blew the penguins apart.

Their journeys were long and lonely.

Bootsy followed the trail through the rain

and snow

and dreamed of better days.

'I hope I will see you again,' thought Penguin, as he laid out a sign for Bootsy to find.

They knitted peak to peak as the trail of yarn went on and on. They pulled themselves up higher and higher.

Finally . . .

. . . they reached the very top. Penguin and Bootsy had pulled right into each other's hearts.

And together . . .

. . . love was a BIG adventure!

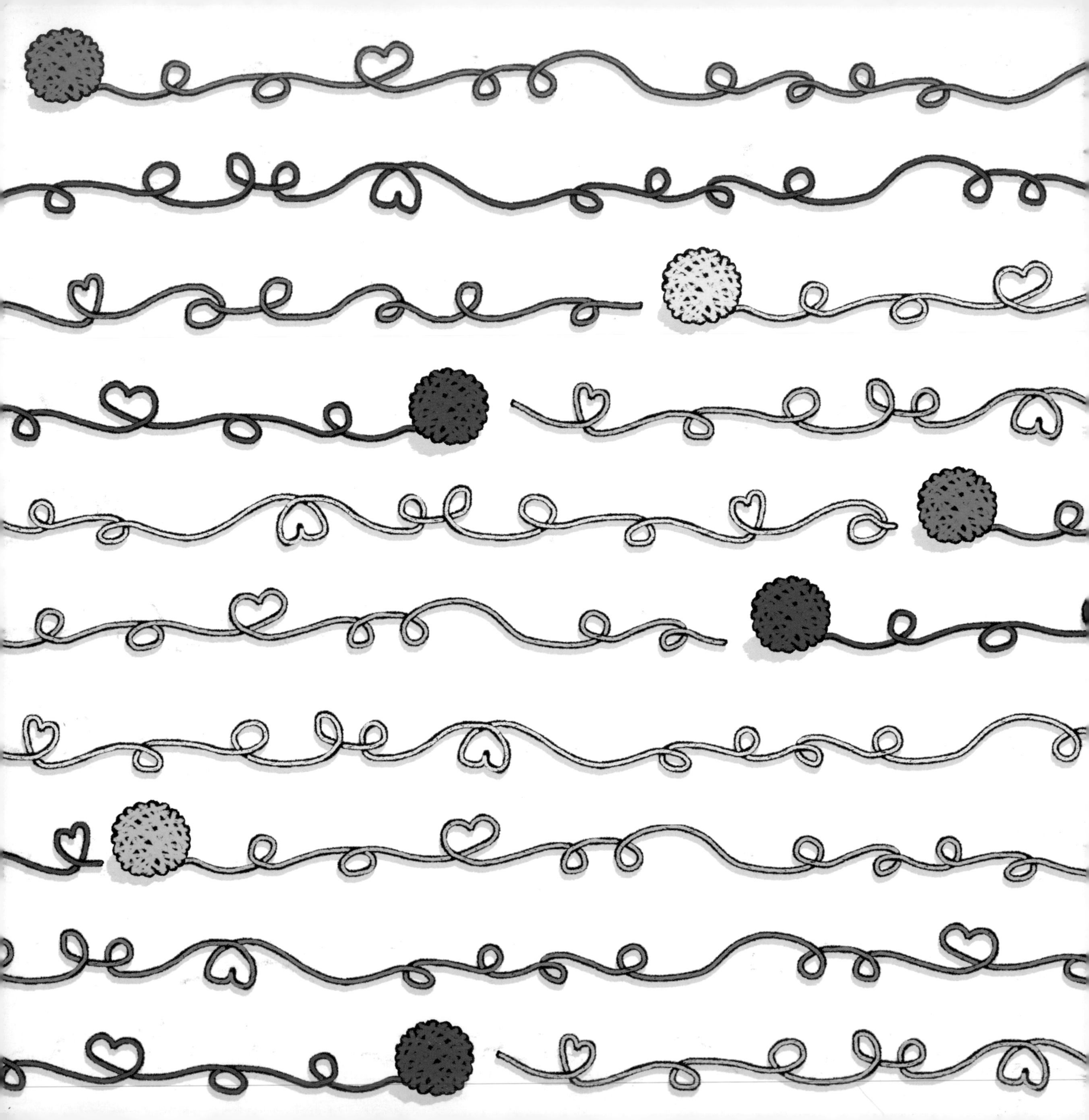

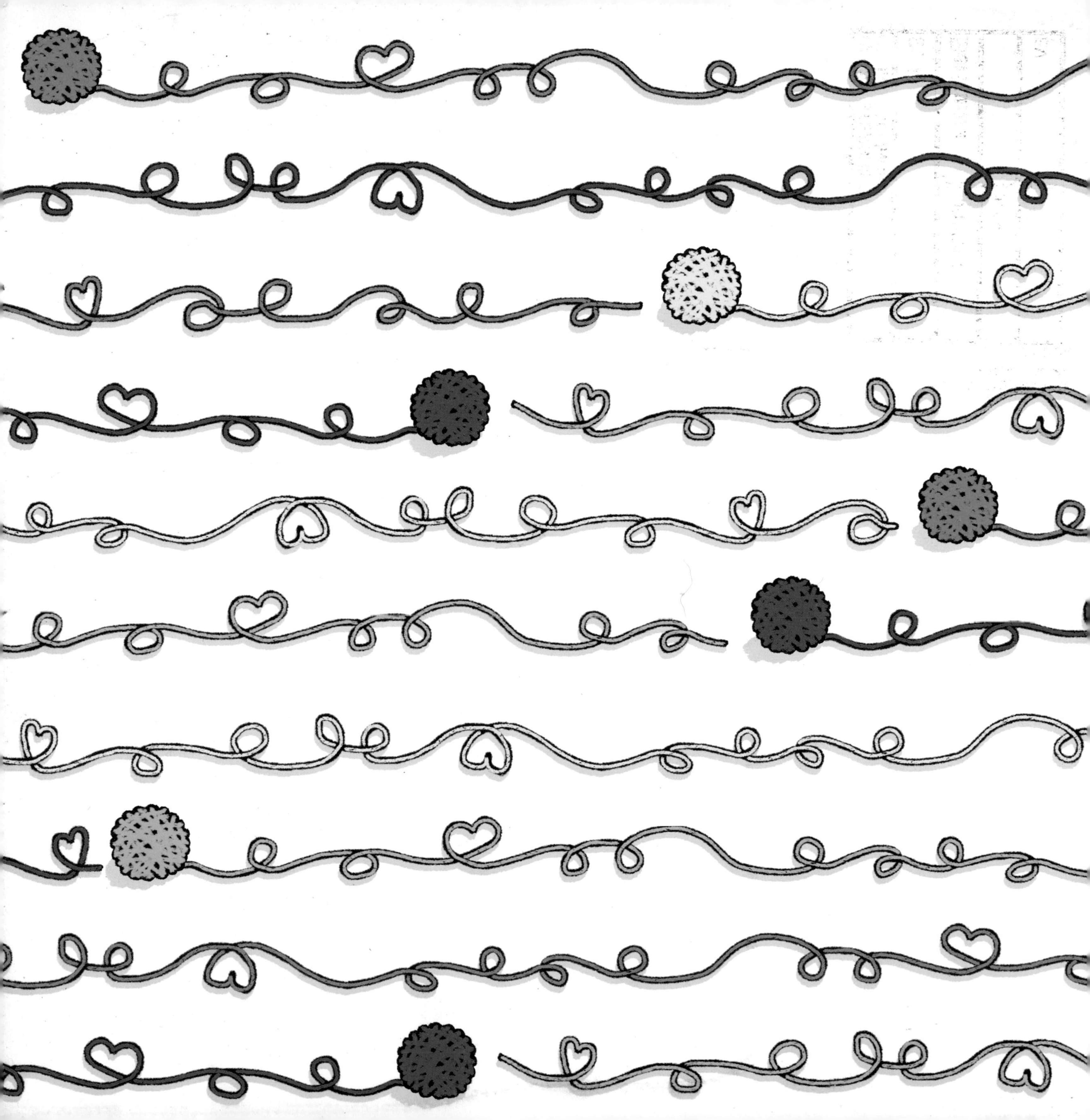

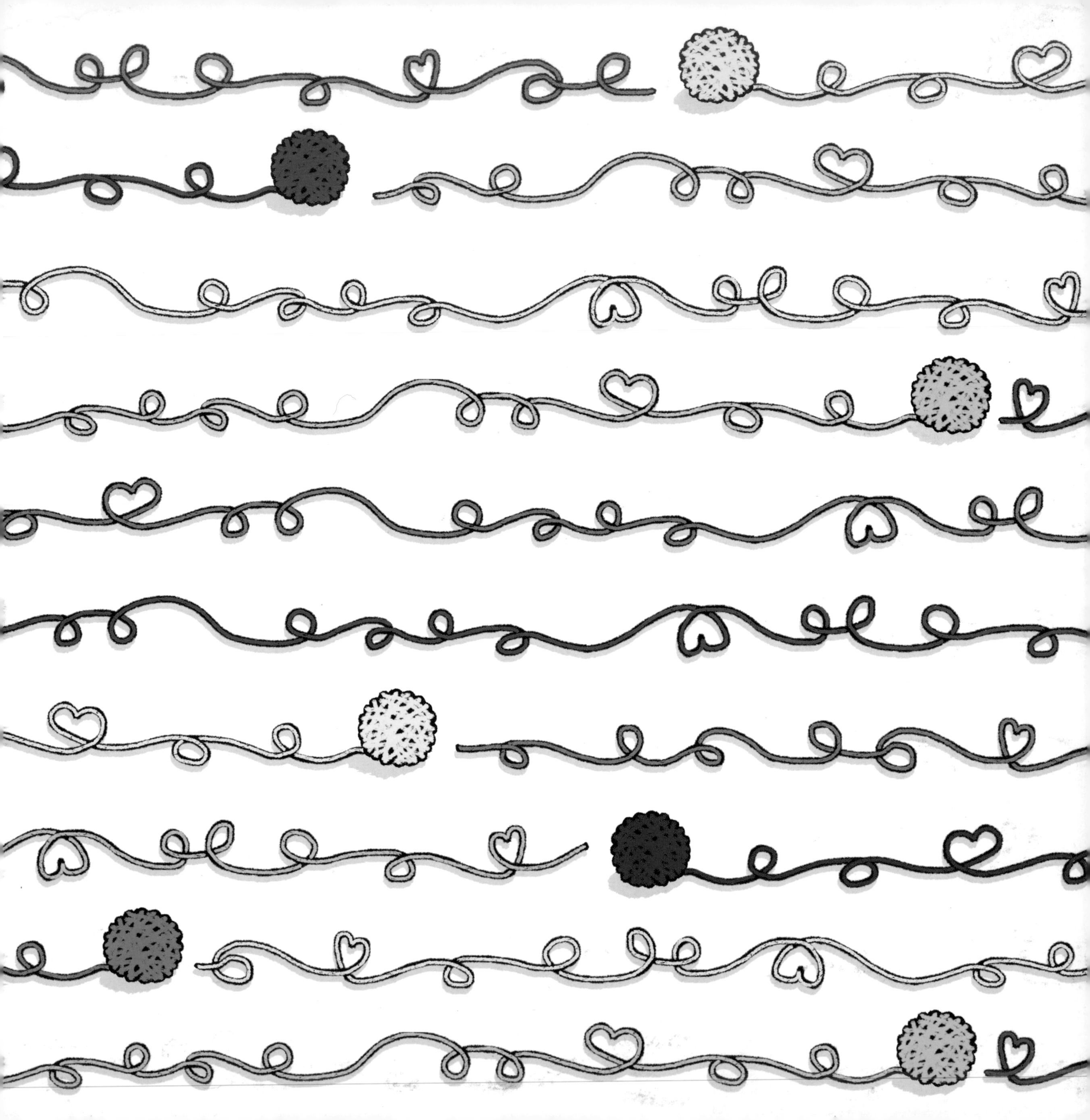